ROCKS AND MINERALS™

Gemstones

Connor Dayton

PowerKiDS press™

New York

Published in 2007 by The Rosen Publishing Group, Inc.
29 East 21st Street, New York, NY 10010

First Edition

Editor: Jennifer Way
Book Design: Greg Tucker
Photo Researcher: Sam Cha

Photo Credits: Cover, pp. 5, 7 (all), 9 (all), 11, 13, 15, 17 (all), 19 Shutterstock.com; p. 5 (inset) © Jeremy Liebman/Getty Images; p. 21 © Dorling Kindersley/Getty Images.

Library of Congress Cataloging-in-Publication Data

Dayton, Connor.
  Gemstones / Connor Dayton. — 1st ed.
      p. cm. — (Rocks and minerals)
  Includes index.
  ISBN-13: 978-1-4042-3686-8 (library binding)
  ISBN-10: 1-4042-3686-4 (library binding)
  1. Precious stones—Juvenile literature. I. Title.
  QE392.2.D39 2007
  553.8—dc22

                                          2006028062

Manufactured in the United States of America

Contents

What Are Gemstones?

Gemstones are valued for their beauty. There are about 100 different kinds of gemstones. They can be almost any color. Gemstones are found all over the world. Almost all gemstones are rocks or **minerals**. A few gemstones are made of **organic** matter. These gemstones are made up of things that were once plants or animals but that have changed and hardened over time.

Most gemstones are cut, smoothed, and used in **jewelry**. Some gemstones can cost a lot of money because they are rare, or hard to find.

These red gemstones are garnets. *Inset:* This is a jeweler working on a ring.

Classifying Gemstones

Scientists classify, or group, gemstones in two ways. They can be classified by what the gemstone is made of. This is called its **chemical composition**. Gemstones are also classified by their crystal system. The crystal system is the way the chemicals in something bond, or stick together, to make up a form.

Gemstones can also be grouped by color. A gemstone called beryl can come in many colors. The different **impurities** that can be mixed in when the rock is being formed give it different colors. Each color of beryl has its own name.

These three gemstones are all beryl. The bixbite is red, emerald is green, and aquamarine is bluish-green.

How Are Gemstones Made?

Most gemstones are made deep inside Earth. It is hot there. Things inside Earth are also under a lot of pressure. Pressure is a force that pushes things together.

Together heat and pressure cause changes to the rocks and minerals. Heat and pressure can change the way different chemicals bond and the type of crystal **structure** that forms. For example, both graphite and diamond are made of carbon. Over time graphite can change into diamond if there is enough heat and pressure to change its crystal structure!

Diamonds and graphite (inset) have the same chemistry but different crystal structures. This makes them very different. Diamond is the hardest mineral on Earth, while graphite is soft enough to be used as pencil lead.

Getting Gemstones

Most gemstones are found in Earth. They are removed from under the ground through mining. People or machines dig deep holes called mines. The rocks and dirt that are dug out from the mines are then sorted through to find gemstones.

Gemstones can be found in other places. Sometimes gemstones can be found in riverbeds. The running water of a river wears away at the land and rocks. This can uncover gemstones from rocks that were once underground. People sort through the dirt and rocks in riverbeds to find these gemstones.

Mines are dug deep into the ground, like this opal mine in Australia. *Inset*: Opals are milky stones that can come in many colors.

Making Them Shine

After they are gathered, gemstones need to be cleaned and prepared before they are used. This is done by people called gem cutters and jewelers. Gemstones are first cut into a shape. The cutting can be done by different machines, based on the gemstone's hardness and the look the gem cutter wants.

Once the gemstone has been cut into a shape, it will be **polished**. This is done using **abrasives** that get finer as the polishing goes on. Both the cut and the polish help the gemstone shine.

This jeweler is working on a gemstone. She is using a tool called a loupe to help her see close up.

Precious Gemstones

You might have heard people talk about **precious** gemstones and semiprecious gemstones. These are not scientific classifications. Instead they are groupings based on the historical value of different gemstones.

There are five precious gemstones. They are diamonds, rubies, sapphires, emeralds, and amethysts. Throughout history they were known as the rarest gemstones. This made them costly. Precious gemstones were highly valued for use in jewelry, such as in the crowns of kings and queens. They are still the best-loved and costliest gemstones used in jewelry.

Here is an emerald set in a gold ring with two diamonds.

Semiprecious Gemstones

There are many more types of semiprecious gemstones than precious gemstones. Many semiprecious gemstones are kinds of quartz but are called by names based on their color. Rose quartz, citrine, and onyx are just a few examples of quartz semiprecious gemstones. Quartz is one of the most common minerals. Examples of other semiprecious stones are opal, topaz, and turquoise.

Both precious and semiprecious gemstones are still used today to make all kinds of jewelry. You might know some of these gemstones from seeing birthstone jewelry. A different stone stands for each month in the year.

Birthstone Chart

January — Garnet

February — Amethyst

March — Aquamarine

April — Diamond

May — Emerald

June — Pearl

July — Ruby

August — Peridot

September — Sapphire

October — Opal

November — Yellow Topaz

December — Turquoise

This chart shows the birthstones for each month of the year. Which is your birthstone?

17

Organic Gemstones

Organic gemstones are made from parts of plants and animals. Two examples of organic gemstones are pearls and amber.

Pearls are organic gemstones that are made by animals called oysters. Sometimes matter that can hurt the oyster gets stuck inside its shell. The oyster coats this matter to keep from getting hurt. Over time that coating can build up into a pearl.

Amber is made from tree sap that has hardened over a very long period of time. Sometimes you can see bugs trapped inside pieces of amber. These bugs died millions of years ago!

Amber is an organic gemstone that is generally a clear orange or yellow color. This piece has the bodies of dead bugs in it. This can give the amber a higher value!

Synthetic Gemstones

Some gemstones are not found in nature at all! These are called **synthetic** gemstones. Some synthetic gemstones **imitate** the color and look of the real gemstone. Cubic zirconia looks a lot like a diamond, but it is not made of the same things as a diamond.

There are also synthetic gemstones that imitate the chemical makeup of real gemstones. People have made synthetics of most of the precious gemstones. These can be made into jewelry. Synthetic diamonds are used as abrasives, and cost much less than real diamonds.

Here is a synthetic emerald. There are synthetics for most gemstones for their use in low-cost jewelry.

Using Gemstones

People have always put gemstones to many uses. Long ago people believed that certain gemstones could make sick people get better. People also used to **crush** gemstones and use them in paints. Lapis lazuli is a semiprecious gemstone that was crushed and made into a deep blue paint.

Today diamonds are used in tools that need to cut through or polish very hard things. In 1960, a ruby was used in the first **laser**. New uses keep being found for gemstones.

Glossary

abrasives (uh-BRAY-sivz) Tiny bits of rock used to rub away at larger bits of rock.

chemical composition (KEH-mih-kul kom-puh-ZIH-shun) The makeup of matter.

crush (KRUSH) To destroy something by pressing.

imitate (IH-muh-tayt) To make something like something else.

impurities (im-PYUR-eh-teez) Pieces of matter in something.

jewelry (JOO-ul-ree) Objects worn for beauty that are made of special things, such as gold and silver, and prized stones.

laser (LAY-zer) A very strong ray of light that is used to cut things.

minerals (MIN-rulz) Natural pieces of matter that are not animals, plants, or other living things.

organic (or-GA-nik) Made from plants or animals.

polished (PAH-lisht) Rubbed until it shines.

precious (PREH-shus) Having a high value or price.

scientists (SY-un-tists) People who study the world by using tests and experiments.

structure (STRUK-cher) Form.

synthetic (sin-THEH-tik) Something that is not made in nature.

Index

Web Sites

Due to the changing nature of Internet links, PowerKids Press has developed an online list of Web sites related to the subject of this book. This site is updated regularly. Please use this link to access the list:
www.powerkidslinks.com/romi/gem/